NORTHERN J. CALLOWAY PRESENTS

SUPER-VROOMER!

WRITTEN BY CAROL HALL

ILLUSTRATED BY SAMMIS McLEAN

CONCEIVED BY NORTHERN J. CALLOWAY

DOUBLEDAY & COMPANY, INC.

GARDEN CITY, NEW YORK

Library of Congress Catalog Number 77-26512

ISBN 0-385-14177-7 Trade
ISBN 0-385-14178-5 Prebound

Text copyright © 1978 Northern J. Calloway and Carol Hall
Illustrations copyright © 1978 Sammis McLean

Hi! I'm Northern J. Calloway. Some of you might know me as "David" from "Sesame Street," and I'd like to tell you a little about the story you're going to read.

First of all, it's a true one. It happened to me and my friends a while ago, when I was your age, and I remember it really well. That's because I'm still using the lessons I learned then.

We were filled with the excitement that comes from working together on something really important to us. We had read about a car race and we were going to enter. There was a lot of planning and building. And we got things done, because we had the energy that comes when you're working hard to be Number One. And that's a very special feeling.

But I learned about an even more special feeling than that. It's the feeling that comes with finding out that winning is something more than just getting a medal. And that things like playing the game and keeping your goals in front of you and sharing with your friends can be even more important than winning. And that, along with all the fun we had, is what I'd like to share with you in this book. So, with the help of Carol Hall, who set this story down in words, and Sammis McLean, who brought it to life with his pictures, I am able to invite you to help build and race the *Super-Vroomer!*

NORTHERN J. CALLOWAY.

I could feel it in my bones.
We were gonna win.

Tommy said so too.

"Jesse," he says, "I can feel it in my bones. I can taste it in my mouth. I got a shiver down my spine that tells me we gonna win this race. This car is a Super-Vroomer! We gonna be the champion racin'-car builders and drivers in the *world*."

"Hogwash," says Sarajane. "Bones. Mouth.
Spine. You sound like you in a TV commercial for aspirin.
You ain't. You in a race. Anyhow, it ain't in your bones.
It's in your wheels. Gimme the hammer."

I hand her the hammer. Nobody'd get nothin' done
around here if I wasn't watchin' careful.

"Sarajane," says Tommy, "don't hogwash me no hogwash. It's in my bones 'cause it's in my mind. Don't you know the brain has powers science ain't even found out about yet? Powers! Like X-rays with super-vitamins stuck on 'em. If somebody know they gonna win and if somebody believe strong enough, the invisible X-ray vibrations from the brain jump out, make a big cloud of energy, and help it happen. This Super-Vroomer gonna *win*. You still with me, Sarajane?"

"Pass the wrench," says Sarajane. (She don't impress too easy.)

Tommy read about the race in the newspaper. The rules were, you had to make your own car. So here was how we did it. First, we had to get an old wooden ironin' board. Not plastic. Not metal. It had to be wood. Tommy say wood so it soak up the energy vibrations and the car go faster.

I say wood so we can put the nails in.

Wooden ones is not easy to find, so that was my job. There was a special reason I was picked.

"Jesse," says Sarajane, "it's mostly grandmas who got the old wooden kind of ironin' boards. You got the grandma, you got the job."

So I went to Grandma and got the wooden ironin' board.

Tommy went to the dump and got the superwheels.

Sarajane went up and down the street
and got the milk crates, the rope, the license plate,
the tin cans, the wire, the pipe, the nails, the boards,
and the cushions.

You ask me, I say Sarajane got invisible
energy vibrations all her own.

Makin' the car took about fifty thousand hours.
But it was easy 'cause we're experts.

The race was bein' held fifty-eight blocks from where we lived. They didn't allow Super-Vroomers on the subway or the bus, so we walked.

And everybody was lookin' at us 'cause
our car was so fine.
"Look at 'em lookin'," says Tommy.

"They noticin' the superwheels."

"They noticin' how you wavin' and pointin' at your ownself," says Sarajane.

When we got to Ninety-third Street it was
crowded. Didn't look like nobody but us had walked.
Everybody was gettin' out of big cars.
And everybody was pullin' out their
little cars.
And some of their little cars looked
awful big to me.
Shiny.
Silver.
Long.
And seemed like *everyone* had superwheels.

We was gettin' ready to practice the steerin'
when a tall dude comes over and says his job is
to inspect our car to make sure it's safe.
We were proud to show him the car.
So we waited while he looked at it.
    First he looked over it. Then he looked under it.
After that he looked at us.

    "I'm sorry," he says, "but your car is not completely
safe. It has no brakes. We can't let you race down that
steep hill without some way of stopping.
In adddition to that," he says, "you have no helmet."

    "Don't worry," says Sarajane. "Their heads is
harder than any helmet you ever saw."

Then I talked.

"We got brakes," I says.

"Where?" asked the inspector.

"Here," I says. I pointed to my shoes."When we want to stop, we put out our feet and scrape."

"I'm sorry, but that doesn't qualify," says the inspector.

And he *did* seem sorry.

You know that feeling when you don't have tears in your eyes, but you got 'em somewhere in your chest? And a lot of mad is mixed up with a lot of sad? Well, that was us.

We stood on the side and watched the race.

Somebody named Brad won.
And he got a medal.

After the race, he was holdin' his medal and
havin' his picture taken by his mama. She had one
of them cameras that does the picture while you there.

Tommy and Sarajane was hangin' around and lookin' down in the mouth, but I was the onliest one that did anything.

"Hey," I says to Brad, "wanna race?"

"I just did," says Brad.

"I know," I says, "and you done pretty good, considerin'."

"Considerin' what?" says Brad.

"Considerin' I wasn't in that race myself," I says.

"What?" says Brad.

"I got powers," I says. "Like X-rays with super vitamins stuck on 'em. With invisible energy vibrations."

"You're on," says Brad.

So we raced.

And raced.

And raced.

Naturally, I won.

Brad got out of his car and looked at me a
long time.
"Do I have to give you my medal?" he says.
"I don't want to."
Then he looked at me some more.
"Your car's fastest," he says.
Now it was my turn to look at him.
"I didn't come for no medal," I says.
"I just came to be the champion racin'-car builder
and driver in the *world*."
So we shook on it.

Anyway, this Brad wasn't such a bad cat.
His mama gave me the picture she took of me
comin' down the stretch in the lead. (Brad didn't want
it, I can tell you that.) And he had his medal, so he
was O.K.

So who won?

Here's how I think. Sometimes winnin' is gettin' a medal. And sometimes it's just plain knowin' you're the best one in the race.

And they ain't always the same thing.

Later, on the way home with the Super-Vroomer, Tommy says, "It's hard to explain why, but when you was comin' down the stretch today, Jesse, I knew we was winners."

"That ain't hogwash," says Sarajane.
They both right.
I could feel it in my bones.

Northern J. Calloway grew up in Harlem and graduated from New York City's High School of Performing Arts. A talented and energetic young performer, he is well known to children and their parents for his role as David on "Sesame Street." His list of dramatic credits is impressive, including the Leading Player role in the play *Pippin*.

Carol Hall is a songwriter who grew up in Abilene, Texas, graduated from Sarah Lawrence College, and now lives in New York City with her children, Susannah and Daniel. She has recorded two albums of her own songs, and her lyrics and music have been sung on "Sesame Street," "Captain Kangaroo," and the Emmy Award-winning "Free to Be...You and Me," which was also a record and a book.

Sammis McLean grew up in Cohasset, Massachusetts, a small town south of Boston. After graduating from the Art Institute of Boston, he lived for a short time in Paris, and then came to New York City, where he has coproduced several films for "Sesame Street." He loves theater, opera, and movies. This is the third book he has illustrated for Doubleday.